JUDY MOODY
SUPER BOOK WHIZ

MEGAN McDONALD

illustrated by Peter H. Reynolds

JUDY MOODY

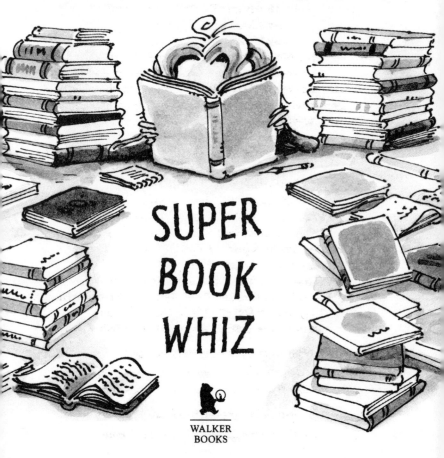

SUPER
BOOK
WHIZ

WALKER
BOOKS

official stuff

Special thanks to the Felida Elementary 2015 Battle of the Books champs of Vancouver, WA. The Blood Sucking Mustache Defenders inspired Braintree Academy's team name.

First published 2019 by Walker Books Ltd
87 Vauxhall Walk, London SE11 5HJ

2 4 6 8 10 9 7 5 3 1

Text © 2019 Megan McDonald
Illustrations © 2019 Peter H. Reynolds
Judy Moody font © 2003 Peter H. Reynolds

This book has been typeset in Stone Informal

Printed and bound in Great Britain by CPI Group (UK) Ltd

British Library Cataloguing in Publication Data:
a catalogue record for this book is available from the British Library

ISBN 978-1-4063-9160-2

www.walker.co.uk

To Book Quizzards everywhere
M. M.

To Mr and Mrs Hobbs
P. H. R.

Table of Contents

A list of all the book titles, series and authors
mentioned in this book can be found on pages 160–165.

Judy Moody

Bookworm, speed-reader (NOT!)
and quizzard

Dad

The book (endings) thief

Mum

No-books-at-the-dinner-table
enforcer

Stink

Bookworm and
Super Sticky-Note Man

Who's Who

Mr Todd

Coach of the Virginia Dare
Bookworms and co-host of
the Book Quiz Blowout

Frank Pearl

Bookworm and
animal expert

Jessica Finch

Bookworm and inventor of
the Jessica Finch Future Teacher
Reading Game

Mighty Fantaskey

Braintree Academy brainiac
and FOURTH-grader

Judy Longstocking

Books, books, books. Piles of books. Miles of books. Stacks of books. Backpacks of books. Towers of books. Hours of books.

Judy Moody read books on her top bunk. Judy read books in the Toad Pee Club tent. Judy read *The Mousehole Cat* aloud to Mouse the cat. She read *Inspector Flytrap* to Jaws, her Venus flytrap. When she read to Stink's guinea pig, Astro, she could tell he liked *The World According to Humphrey,* even though Humphrey was a hamster.

She, Judy Moody, was a book quiz whiz. A book wizard. A quizzard!

Stink read books, books and more books. He read books on the bus. He read books at karate class. He read books during breaks at Saturday Science Club.

For each book he read, he made sticky notes to help him remember stuff: Spanish words in *Juana & Lucas*, cases solved by Timmy Failure, poems in *Silly Verses for Kids*.

Not only was Stink a super reader, he was as fast as lightning on the buzzer. *Bzzz!* He practised at breakfast. *Bzzz!* He practised in the back seat of the car. *Bzzz!* He practised in the bathtub.

"Just think, Stink. In one week, we'll be at the Starlight Lanes Bowling Alley facing off in the first ever Book Quiz Blowout for Virginia Dare School."

"The Bookworms rule!" Stink held his hands high in the air.

"Yeah we do!" Judy double-high-fived Stink. "But the other team is going to be pretty hard to beat."

"We already won three games. We beat all the other second- and third-grade teams at our school!" Stink bragged. "We're undefeated!"

"Not exactly, Stink. We only won that last game because the other team ... you know ... had to ... forfeit."

"Oh, yeah! Some kid barfed his answer and ran to the bathroom and he was too pukey to get back in the game!"

Judy made a yuck face. "Don't remind me."

"We still have a gazillion books to read by Saturday," Stink told Judy.

"Two gazillion," said Judy. "We have to read as many books as we can from Book Quiz Master Lists One and Two."

She was hanging her head upside down off the edge of her bed, reading *Pippi Longstocking.*

"Why are you reading upside down?" asked Stink.

"Pippi does this! Just call me Judy Longstocking. It's a fact that if all the blood rushes to your head, it helps your brain."

"Says who?"

"Says fellow Bookworm Jessica A. Finch."

"I think it would be better to have a superpower," said Stink. "One where you can hold a book up to your head and all the words fly right into your brain."

"Rare!" said Judy without looking down from her book.

"Brainstorm!" said Stink. He ran to his room and came back wearing the cape from his Super Stink costume. Sticky notes were stuck all over his cape. "Super Sticky-Note Man to the rescue!"

Just then, Dad called up the stairs. "Dinner time!"

Judy and Stink ran downstairs with books under each arm. Sticky notes flew from Stink's cape like a trail of bread-crumbs.

"This is new," said Mum, noticing Stink's cape.

"Like it? I'm making sticky notes about all the books I read. To help me remember stuff. I call it the Cape of Good Answers." Stink opened *El Deafo*

and turned to chapter eight.

"Sorry. No books at the dinner table," said Dad.

"But I have to find out what happens to El Deafo at the sleepover."

"Dad's right," said Mum. "I'm all for reading, but this is our time to talk as a family."

"We have to keep reading to be ready for the Book Quiz Blowout!" said Judy.

"Our team, the Virginia Dare Bookworms, is up against the Bloodsucking Fake-Mustache Defenders in the BQB, Book Quiz Blowout."

"That's an unusual team name," said Dad.

"And get this. They're from Braintree Academy," said Judy.

"They even have *brain* in their school name," said Stink.

"Mr Todd told us that all the team names at their school had to be based on a book that was on the reading list. There was a book on the last list called *Fake Mustache*, about a kid who gets a fake moustache. For real."

Stink reached behind his neck and

pulled off a sticky note. "The Heidelberg Handlebar Number Seven!" said Stink. "With the fake moustache, he can rob banks and stuff."

"He even becomes president," said Judy.

"It's great to see you kids so into reading," said Dad.

"You've both been reading up a storm for weeks," said Mum. "I think you're going to do great."

"I hope so. Our whole team has been reading like crazy," said Judy. "Frank Pearl read all the animal books on the list and Sophie of the Elves read all the fantasy books."

"And You-Know-Who read *Charlotte's*

Web three times!" said Stink.

"Jessica Finch," said Judy. "She loves pigs. And guess what. If we can beat Braintree, we win the Book Quiz Wizard's Cup for our school."

"It lights up!" said Stink.

"Sounds like you have a good chance at a trophy," said Mum.

"Webster's family owns the Starlight Lanes Bowling Alley, and he says everybody gets to go bowling and have a bottomless-taco party after! They even have mini pancake tacos with ice-cream filling. No lie."

"What, no Cockroach Clusters and Chocolate Frogs?" asked Judy.

"Nope. Wait, what's that?" Stink asked.

"Wizard food," said Judy. "Or should I say *quizzard* food."

"Eww. Teeny-tiny pancake tacos are way better," said Stink. "And all the money that the bowling alley makes that day will go to buy new books for our school libraries."

"Now do you see why we can't stop reading?" asked Judy.

"I do," said Mum, laughing. "But for now, how about if you focus on eating your turkey burger."

"Super Sticky-Note Man is going in!" Stink took a big bite of turkey burger. Judy sneaked a peek at *Tales of a Fourth Grade Nothing* under the table.

"Hey! No fair! Judy's reading under the table!"

"Stink!" said Judy. "Stop telling on me. Don't you want to win?"

"If I catch you reading at the table again," said Dad, "guess what I'm going to do?"

"Send her to her room without supper!" said Stink.

"Something much worse," said Dad.

Gulp!

"I'm going to rip out the last page of that book, so you'll never know the ending," Dad said, with a tilt of his eyebrow and a rascally grin.

"Nooooo!" Stink cried. "What if the last page holds the answer to the winning question in the Book Quiz Blowout?"

Judy crossed her heart. "I promise I'll wait till after dinner to read."

"Good," said Mum. "But Dad was just kidding. Weren't you, Dad?"

"Of course. I'd never really rip up a book," said Dad, still teasing a bit.

After dinner, the whole family took turns reading aloud from *Charlotte's Web*, right up to the hold-your-breath chapter when Wilbur was on his way to the fair.

"Bedtime," said Mum.

"No fair!" said Stink. They climbed the stairs to their rooms.

"No reading ahead," Judy called downstairs. Mum and Dad cracked up.

Under the covers, Judy read *Tales of a Fourth Grade Nothing* by torch-light. Stink read *The Mousehole Cat* by moonlight.

Judy and Stink read books every spare minute, from *Funnybones* to *Fantastic Mr Fox*, *The Princess and the Crocodile* to *Charlie and the Chocolate Factory*.

They read books from the library. They read books from Mrs Soso's garage sale. They read books from the Little Free Library in front of Fur & Fangs.

A Bookworm Is Not a Worm

At school, third-grade Bookworms Judy Moody, Frank Pearl and Jessica Finch were allowed to miss journal writing to read Book Quiz books in the school library.

Just as Fudge was about to swallow Peter's pet turtle, Stink came rushing over to the Bookworms' table with Sophie of the Elves. "You're never going to believe what just happened!" Stink said, out of breath.

"You finished *Tom Gates: Dog Zombies Rule*?" asked Jessica.

"You finished *Flat Stanley and the Magic Lamp*?" asked Frank.

"You finished *Eight Class Pets Plus One Squirrel Divided by One Dog Equals Chaos*?" asked Judy.

"No!" cried Stink. "Wait. That's not even on Master List One or Two."

"I know," said Judy. "That was a test. You passed."

"Anyway, I was walking back to class from Music," said Stink, "and some fifth-graders called me a bookworm."

"You *are* a Bookworm," Judy pointed out. "That's the name of our team."

"But they said *bookworm* like it's a bad thing!"

"Stink's right," said Sophie. "I heard it too. Especially the worm part."

"Bookworms aren't even worms," said Jessica. "They're actually insects that munch on books. Like the deathwatch beetle."

"At least they didn't call you a death-watch beetle," said Sophie.

"Ignore them, Stinkworm," said Judy. "They're just jealous because you're on the winning team."

"Bookworms are cool, Stink. Why else would there be so many posters about them?" Frank pointed to the front wall of the library.

KEEP CALM AND BE A BOOKWORM

BOOKWORMS RULE THE WORD!

TAKE A BITE OUT OF A BOOK

"Mrs D said Sophie and I could stay in the library to read for Book Quiz too," Stink said. "What book should I read next?"

"Here's a good one," said Judy. "It's about two bad rats."

Stink opened *The Infamous Ratsos*. He turned the page. He cracked up when the Ratso brothers took turns spitting on the playground to look tough. He turned another page. He cracked up some more when they shovelled snow to play a trick on Mr O'Hare, and it backfired.

He turned another page and spotted a bookmark. "Hey! Look what I found in this book." Stink waved a two-dollar bill in front of Judy's face.

"Mine!" said Judy, trying to grab it.

"Is not," said Stink, holding it out of reach.

"Is too! I'm the last one who checked that book out."

"OK, then what's on the back?" Stink asked.

"Um, an eagle. No, wait. A president. No, wait. Eagle."

"Wrong!" said Stink.

"Drat. I thought I fooled you," said Judy. "That two-dollar bill is way rare."

"It has to be worth at least three dollars," said Stink.

"You'd better go show Willa, the new librarian," said Jessica Finch.

"Show me what?" asked Willa, passing by their table.

"Stink found rare money in a library book," said Jessica.

"It's just a two-dollar bill," said Stink.

"Must be your lucky day," said Willa. "The only money I ever found was Monopoly money. But I have found some strange things in books over the years."

"Really?" asked Stink. "Like what?"

"Hmm. Let's see. I've found a lottery ticket, a key, a bubble-gum comic strip, a recipe for macaroni cheese, fortune-

cookie fortunes, half a taco shell, a piece of bacon and baloney."

"Bacon for a bookmark!" said Stink.

"And baloney!" said Sophie, giggling.

"Not too long ago I found a snowflake in a *Mrs Pepperpot* book," said Judy.

"Didn't it melt?" asked Frank.

Judy flipped to page fifty-seven and pulled out a paper snowflake.

"All I ever found in a library book," said Frank, "was a squished bug."

"Yesterday when Jessica was checking books in for me," said Willa, "she found something interesting. Tell them, Jessica."

"I found a letter," said Jessica. "Not just any letter. A love letter!"

"Whoa! Can we see it?" asked Stink and Sophie.

"Sure. Why not?" said Willa. Jessica followed Willa to her office. When Jessica came back, she unfolded a piece of pink notebook paper. "I know who wrote it."

"Who?" asked Frank. "Tell us!"

Jessica Finch made sure nobody else was listening. "I think it was Mr Todd," she whispered.

"Mr Todd? Our teacher, Mr Todd?" asked Judy. "Mr Todd of Class 3T?"

Jessica nodded. She showed them the note and read it out loud. "Roses are red, violets are blue, you look like a krayon, and you act like one too."

"Gross," said Stink.

"No way did Mr Todd write that," said Judy.

"Remember when Ms Tater came to our class? She wrote a book about crayons. Then we found out that she was Mr Todd's girlfriend."

"No way," said Judy. "One, Mr Todd does not write on pink smelly paper. Two, Mr Todd does not write like a second-grader. No offence, Stink. Three, Mr Todd would never spell *crayon* with a *k*."

"I think Judy Moody, Girl Detective, is right," said Frank. "Especially the spelling thing."

"I rest my case," said Judy.

Stink pushed back his chair and got up to go. "Stink, where are you going?" Sophie asked. "You haven't finished your book yet."

"I'm hungry," said Stink.

"But we still have twelve and a half minutes of library time," said Sophie.

Stink headed straight to the chapter-book section. "Yeah, but maybe somebody left bacon in a book," said Stink. "Or a taco. Or baloney!"

Unicorns Don't Wear Trousers

The next day after school, Stink found Judy sitting crisscross applesauce on the floor of her room, flipping the pages of *The Princess in Black* lightning-fast. He was eating a slice of cold pepperoni pizza.

"Want some?"

Judy didn't look up. Flip, flip, flip. She kept turning pages.

"Check this out," said Stink. He put down the pizza. He held out his new

T-shirt for her to see. It said: I READ PAST MY BEDTIME. But Judy did not look up.

He tried to get her attention with a fidget spinner. But Judy did not look up. He spun it in his hand. He spun it on his nose. She still did not look up. Not one fidget.

Something was strange. Something was weird. Something was not right. Her eyes were going batty. Her eyes were going bonkers. Her eyes were going cuckoo-crazy. Judy seemed to be reading, but her eyes were darting up and down like a googly-eyed pet rock. She kept flipping pages like a mad scientist.

"What are you doing?" Stink asked. He took another bite of cold pizza.

"I'm trying to read three-and-a-half times faster than I do now," said Judy.

"Speed-reading?" said Stink. "You mean you can learn to read supersonic fast? Just like that?"

"Yep. Speed-reading is a real thing, you know. Lots of presidents were speed-readers. John F. Kennedy and Jimmy Carter could both read more than one thousand words a minute!"

"I know for a fact that George Washington was not a speed-reader."

"Why not?"

"He must have been a super-slow reader because he had a library book that was overdue for two hundred and twenty-one years."

Judy cracked up. "What?!"

"They said the late fine would have added up to three hundred thousand dollars."

"See? George Washington could have saved himself a ton of money if he had just taught himself to speed-read."

"Yeah, then it wouldn't have taken him more than two hundred years to read the book."

"Guess what," said Judy. "There's a for-real speed-reading champ named Anne Jones who read Harry Potter Book Seven in forty-seven minutes."

"That sounds made up," said Stink.

"For real. No lie!"

"Yeah, but I bet she's a grown-up. No way a kid could do that."

"I heard about a fourth-grader who can read forty-one pages in thirty seconds."

"Whoa," said Stink.

"Pretty soon, I'll be reading at the speed of light. Then I'm going to teach Grandma Lou. That way, she can finally read the longest Harry Potter book and cross it off her before-she-dies bucket list."

"Sweet," said Stink. "Can you teach me, too?"

"Sure," said Judy. "So, right now you probably read a book word by word, one sentence at a time, right?"

"Uh-huh. How else would I do it? Putting a book under your pillow and hoping the words fly into your brain sure doesn't work."

"Don't read word by word any more."

"Huh?"

"Read in 'jumps'."

"How does jumping up and down make you read faster?"

"No, jumps are like chunks of words. It lets your brain take in more words all at once."

"I don't get it," said Stink.

"Think of a tree. When you look at a tree, do you see every leaf or a whole tree?"

"A whole tree," said Stink.

"Speed-reading is like that. You look at a whole page at once instead of looking at one word at a time. Here, I'll show you. Take your finger and run it down the middle of the page. Make your eyes go down the page at the same speed as your finger. Whatever you do, don't go back. That will slow you down."

Judy handed Stink her book. He took his finger and ran it down the middle of the page. His finger left behind a bright-orange greasy mark.

"Stink! You just got pizza all over a library book."

"Oops," said Stink.

"This is worse than the time Ramona

scribbled in Beezus's library book. You're going to have to pay for a whole new book, you know."

Stink shuddered. "Here, I can fix this." He grabbed Judy's pencil with a troll-doll eraser on the end. He started to erase the orange mark.

"Stink! That's not an eraser. That's a troll pencil topper—"

Rrrip! The page ripped.

"Uh-oh," said Judy. "You just made it worse."

"Uh-oh," said Stink. "There goes that two-dollar bill I just found. Unless ... I could just never return the book and it would be overdue for like two hundred and twenty-one years."

Judy held her hand to her ear like a phone. "Hello, Jail," she said, "this is Stink."

"Hardee-har-har," said Stink.

Judy Moody, Speed-Reader,

went back to reading at the speed of light. "Check it out. I bet I can read this whole book in under three minutes."

"What are you reading, anyway?" Stink asked.

"*The Princess in Black*," said Judy.

"What's it about?" asked Stink.

"It's about … um … a princess," said Judy. "And she … wears black."

"Duh," said Stink.

Judy ran her finger down one page, then another, and another. "OK. I got this. Princess Hot Chocolate lives in Wigtower with a skeleton. No, a monster. No, a blue mobile phone."

"Huh? Let me see," said Stink. Stink took the book from Judy. "Hello! Her name is Princess Magnolia and she drinks hot chocolate with Duchess Wigtower."

"Let me try again." Judy made her eyes go fast. She flipped pages. "A sick bird rang and the broom cupboard jumped the castle wall to put trousers on a unicorn."

"Unicorns don't wear trousers," said Stink, shaking his head. "A monster alarm rang and the princess went into

the broom cupboard to change into her black ninja outfit. Then she climbed the castle wall and jumped on a unicorn."

"Then a flying goat who was afraid of snails ate a ninja named Hornswaggle who had magic toenail clippings that roar," Judy added.

"Flying goat! Hornswaggle! Magic toenail clippings!" Stink couldn't stop laughing. "Um, I hate to tell you this, but speed-reading is not working. You don't have a clue what you're reading."

"Maybe I just haven't learned that part of speed-reading yet," said Judy.

"What part?" asked Stink.

"The part where you remember what you read," Judy said.

"I think you better go back to normal reading," said Stink. "Before Princess Hornswaggle marries a ninja snail inside a flying broom cupboard."

Goldfish Thinking

"ROAR!" said Judy.

Jessica Finch crawled inside the Toad Pee Club tent. She opened her pink Peppa Pig lap-desk and pulled out a pink Peppa Pig pencil. She tapped the pencil three times on her lap-desk. "Meeting of the Bookworms is now called to order."

Judy shook Jessica's smiley-face Magic 8 Ball while reading *Anna Hibiscus*. Stink was wearing his Cape of Good Answers, covered in sticky notes.

Jessica peered outside the TP Club tent. "We're missing two Worms."

"Sophie is at her Future Astronomers' meeting," Stink said.

"Frank went to get his glasses checked," said Judy.

"Well, meeting of three-fifths of the Worms is called to order then."

Stink pointed to Jessica's lap-desk. "Isn't Peppa Pig kind of ... preschool?"

"It's for ages three to seven," said Jessica.

"But you're eight, right?" Stink asked.

"Stink," said Judy, "it's a fact that Jessica Finch likes all things pig. Besides, you still play with Mr Potato Head."

"Mr Potato Head is for ages two and up. I'm the up."

"Why are we having a meeting again?" Judy asked Jessica.

"Because we have to eat, sleep and breathe books for the next three days until the big Book Quiz Blowout. I want to be super ready."

"Good thing I made notes," said Stink, pointing to the sticky notes all over his cape. "We can study them. These are the names of the penguins in *Mr Popper's Penguins.* On my back are the names of dogs from books, like Lassie and Winn-Dixie."

Greta

Lassie

I WON THE SMELLING BEE

Jessica read Stink's back. She giggled. "But this one says I WON THE SMELLING BEE."

Stink's face looked like a question mark. "Hey! How did that get there?"

"Smelling bee," said Jessica. "That's a good one."

"Because you smell, Stink. Get it?" Judy asked.

"Fine. I'll call this my Cape of Good Smells."

"C'mon, you guys. Get serious," said Jessica.

"Hey, did you hear?" Judy asked Jessica. "I'm learning to speed-read. Now I can read way more books in the three days we have left."

"Only problem is," said Stink, "she

can't remember anything she reads. Sticky notes help me remember."

"But what will Super Sticky-Note Man do without his cape? You can't wear that to the real Book Quiz."

"Judy's right," said Jessica. "No notes or cheat sheets or visual aids allowed. That's the rules. Anyhoo, I made up a new game to help us get ready for Saturday. You have to guess really fast without using sticky notes." She took out a tray that was covered with a towel. "Under the towel, there are different objects—"

"I love the Tray Game!" said Judy.

"Ooh, I'm good at this," said Stink.

"But it's not the Tray Game," said

Jessica. "It's the Jessica Finch Future Teacher Reading Game. I invented it."

"Huh?" said Stink.

"Everything on the tray has a connection to one of the books we had to read for the Book Quiz Blowout. Each one is a clue. I'll hold up an object. You be the detectives and tell me what book it's connected to."

"Cool beans!" said Judy. "I'm a good detective."

Jessica reached under the towel and pulled out the first object.

"A black and white cat eraser? That has to be—" Judy started.

"The Mousehole Cat!" Judy and Stink called out at the exact same time.

"Too easy. I have to find a harder clue," said Jessica. She reached under the towel. "Ta-da!" In her hand was a ball of squishy red wax. The kind of squishy red wax that used to have cheese inside.

"Cheese wax!" screeched Judy. "From the Ivy and Bean books. Ivy and Bean save up money so they can buy fancy wax-covered cheese for their school lunches. Then they can make moustaches and unicorn horns out of the wax, like the other kids."

"That's loony," said Stink.

"Judy's right," said Jessica. "It's from the Ivy and Bean book *No News Is Good News*."

Next, Jessica pulled out a toy shark.

"There's a submarine shaped like a

shark in one of the Tintin books," said Stink.

"That's right!" said Jessica. "But what is the title of the book?"

"It's … *Tintin and the Lake of Sharks*," said Stink.

"Good answer!" said Jessica.

Jessica reached under the towel again. Judy and Stink couldn't wait to see what would be next.

"Is that … a cherry pit!" said Stink. "Is it a book about George Washington or something?"

"Or something," said Judy. "Give us a hint."

"OK. It's something that a character likes to bake."

Judy twirled the stray piece of hair that

always fell over her eye. Stink chewed his thumb nail.

"It's Princess Peony, the cherry pie princess!" said Judy mid twirl. "She's great at baking cherry pies and hits the Hag of Scrabster's Hump on the nose with a cherry pit!"

"Correct!" said Jessica. "Wow. You guys are good at this."

Stink bounced on his heels. "What else is under there?"

Jessica pulled out a clock.

A clock! Judy tried to think of a book with a clock in it. Stink stared at the clock. They thought and thought. Stink squinted his eyes. Stink scratched his head. Stink made fish lips.

"Stink, what are you doing?" asked Judy.

"I'm trying to concentrate like a goldfish," said Stink.

"Like a goldfish?" asked Judy and Jessica.

"Sure, why not? The average person has an attention span of seven seconds. But a goldfish has an attention span of eight seconds."

Judy tried to concentrate like a goldfish, too.

"Wait a second," said Judy. "What if clock is not the tick-tock kind of clock. What if it's a name, like the last name of the Borrowers!"

"Arrietty Clock! That's the name of the

main character," said Stink.

"Exactly!" said Jessica, clapping her hands.

"That's some good goldfish thinking," said Stink.

"Thanks!" said Judy.

"I could play this game all day," Stink told Jessica. "Any chance you brought meatballs for one of the clues? Because the answer would be *Cloudy with a Chance of Meatballs*. And we could eat the clue!"

"Good thinking, Stinkerbell," said Judy.

"There's one more clue," said Jessica. She reached under the towel and pulled out ... nothing! She held out her hand, but there was nothing in it. No thing.

"Any guesses?" she asked.

"There's nothing there," said Judy.

"Exactly! *Tales of a Fourth Grade Nothing*! Get it?"

Judy smacked her forehead. "That's the book I'm always reading."

"No way. That's impossible to guess!" said Stink. "Even a fourth-grader would not be able to guess that clue."

Just then, they heard voices outside the tent. "Knock, knock!"

"Who's there?" asked Judy.

"The Bookworms!"

"C'mon in!" said Jessica. Sophie and Frank ducked into the TP Club tent.

"Now that we're all here," said Judy, "what if we try a new game? Let's see how many kinds of candies and sweets we can remember from *Charlie and the Chocolate Factory*."

"Marshmallow pillows!" said Sophie.

"Roast-beef chewing gum," said Frank.

"Candy-coated pencils," said Judy. "And lickable wallpaper."

"Ice mice," said Frank.

"Ice mice are from Harry Potter," said Jessica.

"Oops!"

"Mint jujubes," said Sophie. "They turn your teeth green for a month."

"Hair Toffee!" said Stink. "It makes your hair grow like Bigfoot's."

"Rainbow drops," said Jessica. "You'll spit in six different colours."

"Don't forget luminous lollies," said Sophie. "They're lollipops that you eat in bed at night."

"Rare!" said Judy. "I bet we got them all."

"And I didn't even have to look at my sticky notes," said Stink.

"We are all over this like cold on ice," said Sophie.

"Like cold on ice mice!" said Frank.

"Here we come, Bloodsucking Fake-Mustache Defenders!" said Judy.

Brain Freeze

After school on Thursday, Mr Todd lined up the Virginia Dare Bookworms in the front row of Class 3T. Stink and Judy sat on either end, like bookends. Sophie, Jessica and Frank were in the middle.

"Welcome, Bookworms," he started. "This is our last official practice before the final Book Quiz Blowout on Saturday. I know you've been working hard. What great readers you all are."

Just then, Mr Todd noticed Stink's cape covered in sticky notes. "Stink, what's all this?" asked Mr Todd.

"This is my Cape of Good Answers. The sticky notes help me remember stuff from the books I read."

"It's his cheat sheet," said Jessica Finch.

"Nah-uh," said Stink. "Think of it like a study aid."

"I can see how notes might be helpful for studying," said Mr Todd. "But you'll have to get through this practice session without them."

"Stink, you won't be able to use notes at the real Book Quiz," Sophie reminded him. "So think of this as a dress rehearsal."

"You mean undress rehearsal," said Stink. He took off his cape and handed it to Mr Todd.

"OK, team. You've eaten up all the books on the reading list like bookworms. Just do your best. If you can't think of an answer, don't panic. Take a deep breath and try again."

Mr Todd took out a list of practice questions. "Here we go, Bookworms. Sophie, let's start with you."

"Wait," said Stink. "Where's the buzzer?"

"We won't be using buzzers today," said Mr Todd, "so we can focus on the questions and answers."

"Aw, no buzzers!" Stink slunk down in his chair.

Mr Todd cleared his throat. "In *The 13-Storey Treehouse* by Andy Griffiths and Terry Denton, there is a machine that follows you around and shoots *what* into your mouth whenever you are hungry?"

"Marshmallows!" said Sophie. Mr Todd nodded.

"Jessica Finch, what animal that is not a pig befriends Mango Allsorts in *Mango and Bambang* by Polly Faber?"

"A tapir," said Jessica Finch, who knew all things pig and not-pig.

"That is correct."

"Judy, in *Diary of a Spider*—"

"Fly! Grandparents' Day! Itsy Bitsy Spider!" Words from *Diary of a Spider* sputtered out of Judy like popcorn popping.

"Judy, please slow down and wait until you hear the question. Ready?"

Judy took a deep breath.

"In *Diary of a Spider* by Doreen Cronin, Grampa spider suggests that butterflies taste better when eaten with what?"

Judy sprang up from her seat. "Not ketchup. Not mustard. Barbecue sauce!"

"Correct!" said Mr Todd.

"Frank, in *Emil and the Detectives* by Erich Kästner, what is the name of the bank robber that Emil and his friends chase across Berlin?"

"We just read this. It's…" Frank snapped his fingers three times. "Mr Grundeis."

"Good for you," said Mr Todd.

"Stink, your turn. In the Lulu series

by Hilary McKay, Lulu takes an egg to school. What does it become when it hatches?"

Bzzz. Stink made a buzzer sound. Then, nothing.

Judy looked over at Stink. Something was not right. Something was wrong.

He looked like he had just swallowed a fly. His eyes looked like a robot's. Or a zombie's. Zombie robot! Oh, no! This could only mean one thing...

Brain freeze!

Judy had to help Stink snap out of it. The clock was ticking...

Stink looked around in a panic, hoping to take a peek at the Cape of Good Answers. He saw Judy instead, madly flapping her arms at her sides.

"Stink?" asked Mr Todd. "Are you with us?"

Stink's eyebrows shot up. "A duckling! Weep, weep, weep!" said Stink, imitating a baby duck.

"That is correct," said Mr Todd. "But

I'm afraid you took too much time, so the Bookworms would not have got the ten points."

Judy whispered to Frank. "Tell Stink to shake it off." Frank whispered to Jessica. Jessica whispered to Sophie. Sophie whispered to Stink.

Stink started to cough. He stuck out his tongue. His face turned red.

"Need some water, Stink?" asked Mr Todd.

"I'm OK. Judy told me to fake a cough."

"I said 'shake it off', not 'fake a cough'."

The Bookworms cracked up.

Mr Todd asked the Bookworms questions and more questions. But every time it came around to Stink, the same thing happened.

"Stink," said Mr Todd. "In *My Father's Dragon* by Ruth Stiles Gannett, name three things that Elmer Elevator takes with him to Wild Island to rescue a baby dragon."

Brain freeze! Stink was blanking without his Cape of Good Answers.

Judy could think of five things. Chewing gum! Lollipops! Hair ribbons! Rubber bands! Magnifying glass! For sure Stink could come up with three.

But Stink still had icicles on the brain. Without his cape, Super Sticky-Note Man had lost his superhero powers.

Judy mimed chewing gum and blowing a bubble. She pretended to lick a lollipop.

She acted out tying a ribbon in her hair. But Stink didn't notice a thing. He had his eyes closed.

"Excuse me," said Jessica Finch, "but Judy's a cheater pants. The rules are you can't help another team member."

"Judy, no helping your brother, please," said Mr Todd. "That would get your team a wrong answer."

"But this is just practice," said Judy. "And it's not like it helped him any."

All of a sudden, Stink opened his eyes. He seemed to snap out of it. He was not a robot. He was not a zombie. He was Encyclopedia Stink again.

"Chewing gum, rubber band, magnifying glass," said Stink.

"Stink, you did it!" said Judy. "I didn't even help him. Honest, Mr Todd. Some of those were not even the words I was acting out."

"Stink, did you come up with the answers all on your own?" asked Mr Todd.

"Yes!" said Stink. "Honest to ice cubes! I just closed my eyes and pictured my sticky notes. Then all of a sudden my brain freeze melted and I knew the answers!"

"I'm glad your brain freeze finally melted, Stink," said Sophie.

"Me too," said Judy. She pointed to the floor under Stink's

chair. "But now there's a big wet puddle under your chair."

"What?" cried Stink. He leaned over and peered under his chair.

"Made you look!" said Judy.

Grumpy Bacon

Friday came – the last day before the Book Quiz Blowout. All day at school, the clock did not seem to move. Judy began to think she knew just how Ivan the gorilla felt, pacing in his cage at the Exit 8 Big Top Mall in *The One and Only Ivan.*

She could hardly wait to get home and practise one last lightning round with

Stink. But when she hopped on the bus, Stink wasn't on it.

At home, Judy ran upstairs. Stink was lying on his race-car bed, up to his neck in covers, with a thermometer sticking out of his mouth.

"Stinkerbell!" said Judy. "You're sick?"

Judy ran to get her Elizabeth Blackwell doctor kit. "Stink, this is worse than Pippi Longstocking having a major case of the freckles. What do you have, anyway?"

"Grumpy," said Stink. "Bacon."

Grumpy! Bacon? Oh, no! Stink had measles of the mouth. Chickenpox of the brain. He couldn't even talk right!

Stink took the thermometer out of his mouth. "The school nurse says I have

a sensitive stomach," said Stink. "That means tummy-ache."

"Oh!" said Judy. "I thought you said grumpy bacon."

"Not even. It feels more like Ping-Pong ball stomach. Is that a thing?"

"It is when you have a big important Book Quiz coming up," said Judy.

"The good news is, the nurse sent me home early, so I got to read more books," said Stink. "More good news is Mum brought me sick food: ginger ale and buttered toast. Just like—"

"Mercy Watson!" said Judy and Stink at the same time.

"But the bad news is, what if I'm sick for the Book Quiz?"

"I think if we just keep practising, you'll feel better about tomorrow."

Judy dug in her backpack for flash cards. "Lightning round!" said Judy. "Let's see how many questions you can answer in sixty seconds. No peeking."

Judy took out a buzzer and a timer from one of her board games.

"Do I get to buzz in?" Stink asked. "I get to buzz in, right? Because using the buzzer is good for a sensitive stomach."

"Fine." Judy handed over the buzzer. She flipped the timer over. "Go! What's the name of the brave pig in *Charlotte's Web*?"

Bzzz. "Wilbur."

"Who keeps a polka-dot horse on her porch and a monkey named Mr Nilsson?"

Bzzz. "Pippi Longstocking."

"What street do Ramona the Pest and her cat, Picky-picky, live on?"

Bzzz. "Klickety-Klackety Street."

"Sorry, Stink. It's Klick-i-tat Street. Next question: Name three of Horrid Henry's classmates."

Bzzz. "Moody Margaret, Rude Ralph, Sour Susan."

"In *Merci Suárez Changes Gears*, Merci is chosen to be a Sunshine Buddy to the new kid. What's his name?"

Bzzz. "Matthew!"

"Michael! Can you tell me where Michael is from?"

Bzzz. "Minnesota."

"Good. Whose bizarro library has holograms and hovercrafts and a white tiger?"

Bzzz. "Mr Monticello."

"Wrong! Stink! You always say Mr Monticello! It's Mr *Lemon*cello." Judy made a sour-ball face. "Think of sour lemons. Lemonheads. Lemon pie."

Ding-dong. The doorbell rang. Judy ignored it.

"What is Mr Popper's job in *Mr Popper's Penguins*?"

"He paints houses," said fellow Bookworm Frank Pearl, coming into Stink's

room. "I remember because I read all the animal books twice."

"Hey, you can be in the lightning round too," Judy said to Frank.

"Sure. Hit me."

"OK. This one's for you, Frank. Name three enemies of the Oompa-Loompas in *Charlie and the Chocolate Factory*."

"Easy," said Frank. "Whangwangers, snogwogglers and swozzdoodles."

Judy and Stink groaned.

"What?" asked Frank.

"It's whangdoodles," said Judy.

"And hornswogglers," said Stink, cracking up.

"And snozzwangers," said Judy.

Stink cracked up some more. "Ow!" He clutched his sensitive stomach. "Don't make me laugh."

"Are you OK?" asked Frank. "What's wrong with you, anyway?"

"He's going to be fine," said Judy. "He

just has a Ping-Pong ball stomach."

"Wait, what? You swallowed a Ping-Pong ball?" asked Frank. "Cool! Did they take an X-ray?"

"Not a real Ping-Pong ball," said Stink.

"This is just like in Horrid Henry! *Horrid Henry's Underpants* is book number seven on Master List Two. That cheeky Henry faked a tummy-ache to get out of learning his spelling."

"I'm not faking," said Stink. "I have a sensitive stomach."

"It just means he's worried about the contest tomorrow," said Judy.

"When I have a tummy-ache, I eat crackers and drink milk," said Frank. "No, wait. That might be for a headache.

For a stomach-ache, I take a bath."

"A bath!" said Stink. "No way am I taking a bath when I'm not even dirty. How does a bath help, anyway?"

"Oh, wait. Maybe it's take a nap," said Frank. "Not take a bath."

Ding-dong. Doorbell again. This time, Sophie ran up to Stink's room.

"I read every Julius Zebra and I just finished *Grapple with the Greeks*!" Sophie said. "Ask me anything."

"OK," said Judy. "What do Julius and his friends use to defeat the fearsome minotaur?"

"A ball of string!" said Sophie.

"What is the name of Julius Zebra's brother?" asked Stink.

"Brutus!" said Sophie. That's when she noticed that Stink was in bed. "Stink! Are you sick? What's wrong with you?"

Stink said something with the thermometer in his mouth again.

"Grumpy bacon?" Sophie repeated.

"That's what I thought he said, too!" said Judy.

Stink pulled out the thermometer. "Tummy-ache," said Stink.

"I know how to fix a tummy-ache," said Sophie.

"I hope it's not by taking a bath. Or a nap."

"Nope. All you have to do is talk to your tummy-ache."

"No way am I talking to my tummy-ache," said Stink. "I'd feel stupid."

"C'mon, Stink," said Sophie. "You want the Bookworms to win the Book Quiz Blowout, don't you?"

"OK, OK. I'll talk to it. Tummy-ache, get out of here. Now. Begone!"

Stink sat up. Stink took another sip of ginger ale. He smiled a big smile. He looked surprised. "Hey, I think my tummy-ache is gone! For real."

"I think it was the ginger ale," said Judy.

"I think it was the talking," said Sophie.

"Wait, wait! Everybody be quiet for a minute," said Stink. "I think my tummy-ache is talking to me."

"What's it saying?" everybody asked.

"It's saying, 'The Bookworms are so going to crush the Bloodsucking Fake-Mustache Defenders.'"

"Yeah we are!" Judy and Frank and Sophie chimed in.

The Mighty Fourth-Grader

Judy was quizzing the Bookworms about *Tales of a Fourth Grade Nothing* when the doorbell rang. *Ding-dong-ding-dong-ding-dong.* "Sheesh!" said Judy. "You'd think it was Girl Scout cookie time or something."

"Who else could it be?" asked Stink.

"There's only one Bookworm missing," said Sophie.

"Jessica A. Finch!" said Judy. She dropped her book and ran downstairs to answer the door. It was not Jessica Finch.

It was Amy Namey.

Amy Namey, Ace Reporter, rushed through the front door. She had her clipboard under her arm and a pencil behind her ear. "Newsflash," said Amy. "I ran all the way over here to give you the big news in person."

Judy tried to think of really big news. She imagined these headlines:

HURRICANE CAUSES BIG BAD BLACKOUT!

SWARM OF BEES FINDS FROG NECK LAKE!

BIGFOOT SIGHTING ON CROAKER ROAD!

Judy dashed upstairs with Amy. "Listen up, everybody. Amy has big fat news."

"Mr Todd said I could be the reporter for the Book Quiz Blowout. I'm going to write about it for our school paper. I went to Braintree Academy to get a big scoop on the Bloodsucking Fake-Mustache Defenders. Guess what I found out!"

"They all wear fake moustaches?" asked Sophie.

"They're really vampires?" asked Frank.

"And they vant to suck the Bookvorm brains right out of our heads?" asked Judy in her best vampire voice.

"No, no, no. Nothing like that ... I found out ... the other team has..."

"Has the pukes?" asked Stink.

"Has moustaches for real?" Frank asked.

"Has supersonic speed-readers?" asked Judy.

"The other team has a ... fourth-grader!" said Amy in an almost-whisper.

Sophie's mouth dropped open. Stink's eyes got as big as mini pancakes. The room went dead quiet. So quiet you could have heard a page turn.

"Her name is Mighty Fantaskey," said Amy.

Gulp! "Her name is Mighty?" asked Judy.

"What kind of a name is that?" asked Sophie.

"Sounds like a mighty fantastic name to me," said Frank.

"Sounds like a superhero name!" said Stink. "She could be a superhero!"

"Or she could be a fourth-grade nothing," said Judy, holding up her book.

"I didn't meet her," said Amy. "But the other kids on her team say she eats books for breakfast. That means she's a brainiac."

"Stink's a brainiac too," said Sophie. "His superhero name could be Encyclopedia Stink."

"And don't forget Judy's been to college," said Frank.

"Sort of," said Judy. "Mighty Fantaskey knows how to speed-read," said Amy. "They say she can read a whole page as fast as you can turn it."

"That's impossible," said Frank.

"No, it's not," said Stink. "Judy can speed-read. She showed me."

"Not really," said Judy. She hated to admit it.

Amy went on. "They say she reads fifth-grade books, like Harry Potter Book Five. She didn't just carry it around to look cool."

"No lie?" asked Judy.

Amy nodded.

"That's almost nine hundred pages!" wailed Judy.

"No fair," said Stink. "Fourth grade is against the rules."

"That's right," said Sophie. "Fourth-graders are supposed to be on teams with fifth-graders."

"Not exactly," said Amy. "The rule is that you just have to be seven to nine years old to be on the younger team. She's nine."

"Nine!" said Judy. "That's one whole birthday candle more than me."

"And two whole grades more than us!" said Sophie.

Amy looked at her notes. "She was home-schooled till this year."

"Aagh!" said Frank. "That means she's way super smart. She probably read every book in the whole entire library twice."

"Whoa," said Judy. "That's gifted."

"That's not all," said Amy. "She moved here from Royal Oak, Virginia. In Royal Oak, Virginia, Mighty Fantaskey was on a Book Quiz team called the Bookensteins."

"Oh, like Book Einsteins," Judy said in a whisper. "Yipes."

The Bookworms got super quiet again. As quiet as the Ratso brothers eating cheese sandwiches. As quiet as the Borrowers when they hid under the floorboards from the human beans.

"The Bookensteins were undefeated going into finals. Then Mighty moved."

The Bookworms were so quiet you could have heard a Grouchy pencil drop.

"What are we going to do?" asked

Sophie. "The Book Quiz Blowout is in eighteen hours and twenty-three minutes from now."

Ding-dong. Doorbell again? Judy ran downstairs to answer the door. This time it was Jessica Finch. Judy brought her up to Stink's room, where they took turns telling her about the fourth-grader.

"O-nay iggie-bay," said Jessica Finch when they were done.

"Huh?" said Sophie and Stink.

"It's Pig Latin for 'No biggie'," said Jessica. "I'm almost nine and I've read a fifth-grade book before. The Advanced Fifth-Grade Practice Spelling Student Edition."

"But this isn't a spelling bee," said

Judy. "It's a book quiz. And this Mighty girl is some kind of book Einstein."

"And your name's not Mighty," said Stink.

Frank scratched his head. Sophie fidgeted with her glasses. Stink felt his sensitive stomach do a belly flop.

The Bookworms were feeling lousy. They were in a slump. They were down in the dumps. Judy knew a thing or two about bad moods. And she knew a thing or three about how to change them.

"Hey, Bookworms!" said Judy. "We have good stuff on our side, too."

"But we don't have a fourth-grader," said Frank.

"A fourth-grade superhero," said Stink.

"We have something much better," said Judy.

"What could be better than a fourth-grader?" asked Sophie.

"We have the courage of Wilbur and the imagination of Pippi Longstocking. Pippi would say that to win, we have to first be able to imagine winning. Close your eyes, everybody."

The Bookworms closed their eyes. "Now I want you to go to your happy place," said Judy. "Just for pretend. I learnt this when I went to college."

Judy imagined herself on the front porch of Villa Villekulla, the house where Pippi lived with her polka-dot horse and her monkey, under the soda-pop tree.

Jessica Finch splashed in mud at a pig farm. Sophie rode a unicorn. Stink took part in a stinky trainer contest. Frank imagined being at the Fur & Fangs pet shop.

"Now," said Judy, "imagine winning the Book Quiz Blowout."

Jessica saw herself taking a bow in a pink party dress with a swirly skirt. Frank pictured himself holding the light-up Book Quiz Wizard's Cup. Sophie dreamed of tiny elves helping her with answers. Stink, aka Super Sticky-Note Man, flew through a sky full of sticky notes in his superhero cape.

Judy imagined she was Moody Fantaskey, speed-reader of twenty thousand words a minute. "Now open your eyes and repeat after me," said Judy. "We are the Bookworms."

"We are the Bookworms."

"We eat books."

"We eat books."

"We are not endangered!"

"We are not endangered!"

Super Book Whiz

That night, Judy slept in fits and starts.

She dreamed she was the Princess in Black. She dreamed she was El Deafo. She dreamed she was a mighty fantastic fourth-grade wizard. A wizard with the power to fly faster than the speed of speed-reading.

At last it was Saturday. The day of the big Book Quiz Blowout. All morning, Stink could hardly wait for it to be quiz time. It was worse than waiting for Santa

Claus, the Easter Bunny and the Tooth Fairy combined.

At breakfast, Judy read the last chapter of *Tales of a Fourth Grade Nothing*. Stink read the last chapter of David Walliams' *Ratburger*. Dad didn't even rip out the last pages of their books for reading at the table.

"Exciting day, huh kids?" said Mum.

"Do you feel ready for the big quiz game?" asked Dad.

"I feel as strong as Pippi did when she lifted up her horse with two hands. I'm Judy Moody, Super Book Whiz!" Today was going to be mood-tastic!

"And I finally memorized all the names of Mr Popper's penguins," said

Stink. "Want to hear? Captain Cook, Greta, Columbus, Victoria, Nelson, Jenny, Magellan, Adelina, Scott, Isabella, Ferdinand and Louisa."

After breakfast, they got ready to go to the Book Quiz Blowout. Judy dressed up like Pippi Longstocking. She drew freckles on her face and put pipe cleaners in her plaits so they stuck out funny. She wore her lucky high-tops and tucked her lucky penny into her pocket.

Stink dressed as a brainiac – aka himself, minus the Cape of Good Answers.

When they got to the Starlight Lanes, Stink's friend Webster Gomez ran over to them. He was dressed like a worm with glasses and a graduation cap. "I decided to dress like a bookworm. You know, sort of like being your mascot." He held up a printed sign. It read: CONGRATS BOOKWORMS, GRAND CHAMPS. "I made it myself!"

"Thanks," said Stink. "But we haven't won yet." He told Webster all about the Bloodsucking Fake-Mustache Defenders, including the mighty fantastic speed-reading fourth-grader.

"*¡Ay!*" said Webster. "But don't forget, the Bookworms are fantastic too. *¡Buena suerte!* Good luck!"

Webster led them over to the Party Room. The room was abuzz with parents and teachers. And friends like Rocky Zang and Riley Rottenberger and Amy Namey had come with their families. Stink felt a jolt of excitement that made his hair stand up on end.

Two long tables were set with name cards, water glasses and buzzers. Judy and Stink ran to join the rest of the team – Frank, Sophie, and Jessica Finch. Jessica was giving tips for what to do if a team member got nervous.

"And if you feel like you're going to get brain freeze," said Jessica, looking right at Stink, "just tap your nose. It really works."

Judy stole a glance at the Bloodsucking Fake-Mustache Defenders. Their team was wearing matching team T-shirts – all boys and one girl. The girl had a backpack covered with stickers and buttons about reading. Pencils that said READING ROCKS stuck out of the front pocket. Plastic reading charms hung from her zip – a book bug, a reading trophy, a star.

"That must be her," Judy said in a whisper.

Gulp.

"Mighty Fantaskey, the fourth-grader," said Judy.

"Even her shoes look fourth grade," said Frank.

"Check out all her rubber bracelets," said Judy. The girl's arm was lined with bracelets that said things like I HEART READING and KEEP CALM AND READ ON.

Around her neck, she wore metal dog tags on a chain. They jingled when she moved.

"Wow. Look at all her prizes. So many brag tags," said Sophie.

"I bet they say things like STAR READER

and READING ROCK STAR," said Jessica.

"And READING MACHINE," said Judy.

"Have you ever seen so many reading incentives in your life?" asked Jessica.

"I bet that backpack is full of book tokens, too," said Stink.

Jessica nodded. Frank agreed. Despite all the excitement swirling around them, the Bookworms gawked in awe at Mighty Fantaskey, Fourth-Grader.

At last the big match was about to begin!

Book Quiz hosts Mr Todd from Virginia Dare School and Ms de la Cruz from Braintree Academy welcomed everyone. They explained the rules: The two teams would take turns answering

the questions. During a team's turn, the player who buzzed in first got to answer the question. Each correct answer was worth ten points. The next question would then go to the other team and so on. The match would go to one hundred and fifty points.

"To help get us started," said Mr Todd, "I'm going to turn this over to our third-grade newspaper reporter, Amy Namey."

Amy took the microphone. "This is Amy Namey, Ace Reporter, coming to you live from the Party Room of the Starlight Lanes Bowling Alley. It's a showdown between the Virginia Dare Bookworms and the Braintree Bloodsucking Fake-Mustache Defenders. Five students from each school make up the teams that will battle for the Book Quiz Wizard's Cup.

"On the Bookworms' side, we have a fantasy fan, a spelling whiz, a speed-reader, a human encyclopedia and an animal expert.

"On the Braintree team, we have a sports fan, a science champ, a graphic novel maniac and a biography brainiac. And last but not least is a Harry-Potter-reading fourth-grader! But the question of the day is, which team will get to take home the light-up Book Quiz Wizard's Cup to display proudly at their school?"

Amy held up a shiny trophy with a gold cup perched atop a stack of books on a marble base. She pressed a button and

the books lit up in blinking rainbow colours. Everybody *ooh*ed and *aah*ed.

"Thank you, Amy," said Mr Todd.

"Ready to rumble?" asked Ms de la Cruz.

The Fake-Mustache Defenders huddled and did a secret handshake. The Bookworms put their heads together and chanted their motto: "We are the Bookworms. We eat books. We are not endangered!"

A hush fell over the room. The timer was set. The clock began to tick. The official Book Quiz Blowout had begun.

Bookworms v Bloodsucking Fake-Mustache Defenders

The Fake-Mustache Defenders won the coin toss. They got to go first.

"In the book by Andrea Beaty," said Mr Todd, "young scientist Ada Twist tries to figure out the source of a bad smell. Where does she write down her scientific thoughts?"

Mighty Fantaskey buzzed in. "The Great Thinking Hall."

"Correct," said Mr Todd.

"For the Bookworms," said Ms de la Cruz. "What book by author Liz Kessler begins with the line, 'Can you keep a secret?'"

Sophie buzzed in. "*The Tail of Emily Windsnap*."

"Correct. Ten points."

"OK, Fake-Mustache Defenders. From *Charlotte's Web*, by E. B. White, please name one of the words that Charlotte the spider spins in her web."

Mighty buzzed in again. "Terrific. Radiant. Some pig."

"That's three words," said Mr Todd. "But you are correct on all counts. Ten points."

"Bookworms. In *A Series of Unfortunate*

Events by Lemony Snicket, who disguises himself as a sea captain and claims his leg was eaten by leeches?"

Bzzz. "Judy Moody?"

"Count Olaf."

"That is correct. Ten points."

The questions went back and forth, back and forth for several rounds. No one got a single question wrong until the Bookworms could not remember that Domovoi Butler was the bodyguard in the Artemis Fowl books by Eoin Colfer. Then the Fake-Mustache Defenders forgot why Stuart Little left home in the book by E. B. White. *Phew!* After that, Stink said the giant peach landed on the Eiffel Tower, instead of the Empire State Building, in

James and the Giant Peach by Roald Dahl.

"Next question," said Mr Todd. "In *The Story of Tracy Beaker* by Jacqueline Wilson, what name is given to the care home where Tracy lives?"

The boy to the left of Mighty buzzed in. "The Dumpster!" he cried.

"I'm sorry," said Mr Todd. "The correct answer is the Dumping Ground."

The audience groaned. Judy's palms began to sweat. Her fake freckles itched. She took a deep breath to calm herself down.

"In *Because of Winn-Dixie*, by Kate DiCamillo," said Ms de la Cruz, "what is Opal's dog afraid of?"

Every single Bookworm buzzed in.

"Jessica Finch?"

"Thunderstorms," said Jessica.

"Another correct answer for the Book-worms. Add ten points."

"Woo-hoo," yelled Webster from the crowd. Rocky called, "Go, Bookworms!"

The score was tied! The air in the room crackled with electricity.

The Fake-Mustache Defenders knew that poohsticks was the game invented by Pooh Bear and his friends in the A. A. Milne books. Ten more points.

"In Dav Pilkey's *Dog Man*, what kind of creature is Petey?"

Frank buzzed in. "The world's most evil cat!"

Before they knew it, it was half-time,

and the score was eighty to eighty. The two teams were well matched.

"What a game!" said Amy Namey. "The Bookworms and the Bloodsucking Fake-Mustache Defenders are neck and neck. Will the Bookworms take a bite out of the Bloodsuckers? Or will the Bloodsuckers sink their fangs into the Bookworms on their way to the finish and take home the trophy?"

In the second half, the questions got harder. Judy's mouth felt as dry as the desert in *The Little Prince*. She took a gulp of water. She rubbed the lucky penny in her pocket. She clicked the heels of her lucky high-tops together.

"In *Charlie and the Chocolate Factory*,

by Roald Dahl," said Mr Todd, "what happens to Violet Beauregarde when she chews gum against Willy Wonka's wishes?"

Bzzz. "She turns into a giant blueberry," said a Fake-Mustache Defender.

The audience cracked up.

"In C. S. Lewis' *The Lion, the Witch and the Wardrobe*, what queen has cast a spell over Narnia to make it winter for ever?"

"The white witch," said Sophie.

"In a book by Monica Brown, what famous football player is the first man in the history of the sport to score one thousand goals?"

"Pelé, king of football!" said one of the Fake-Mustache Defenders.

"In his picture-book autobiography, what instrument did New Orleans jazz musician Troy Andrews find in the street when he was a boy?"

Bzzz. Stink buzzed in. "A trombone. He's Trombone Shorty."

The rapid-fire questions came one after another. The two teams were still tied, at 140 to 140, with only one question to go for each team!

"Bloodsucking Fake-Mustache Defenders," said Mr Todd. "For ten points, and possibly the game, which London railway station is featured in Eva Ibbotson's *The Secret of Platform 13*?"

One of the Fake-Mustache Defenders buzzed in. The Bookworms held their breath. The place was so quiet you could hear a pin drop, and not the bowling kind of pin. "King's Cross."

"That is correct," said Mr Todd.

The Braintree Academy fans went wild. The Fake-Mustache Defenders screamed like they had just seen Pelé score a goal. The Virginia Dare fans gasped. The Bookworms groaned. If the Bookworms got their last question wrong, the Fake-Mustache Defenders would take home the trophy.

Judy could hear her heart pounding in her ears.

"OK, Bookworms," said Ms de la Cruz. "For the tie, here is your next question. In a novel by Chris Grabenstein, Kyle

Keeley and his cohorts get locked in the unusual library of what famous genius, whose name is part of the book's title?"

Judy tried to ring in first, but Stink beat her to the buzzer. Oh, no! This was the one question he messed up every time. She felt her stomach twist into a knot. She closed her eyes. *Don't say Mr Monticello,* she silently pleaded. She, Judy Moody, was in a sour-ball mood.

"His name…" Stink started.

"Twenty seconds," said Ms de la Cruz, checking the timer.

"Mr…" Stink stopped. He bit his lip, glancing over at Judy, but she wasn't looking at him. Her eyes were squeezed

shut and her face was all pinched, like she had just eaten a lemon.

"Five seconds," said Ms de la Cruz. "We need an answer."

A lemon! Stink practically popped with relief. "Mr Lemoncello!" he said.

"Cor-rect!" said Mr Todd. The crowd erupted in noisy applause.

Judy's eyes popped open in surprise! "Go, Stinkworm!" she cried. "You did it!"

Tie game! The score was even steven –

150 to 150. The Bookworms shrieked and jumped up and down.

The audience went wild. The Blood-sucking Fake-Mustache Defenders sat still, barely blinking.

Amy Namey, Ace Reporter, stepped up to the microphone. "The game is in a dead heat. Ladies and gentlemen, this is a real edge-of-your-seat nail-biter. Now the match will go into a tie-breaking round. We're moments away from having a winner!"

Mr Todd and Ms de la Cruz explained the rules of the Bonus Round. Each team was to choose one player to come up to the microphone with their buzzers. The first player to buzz in with a correct

answer would win the game for their team.

The Fake-Mustache Defenders chose Mighty Fantaskey. The Bookworms chose … Judy Moody, Super Book Whiz!

The pressure was on. She, Judy Moody, did not want to let the team down.

Then it happened.

Mr Todd asked the question: "How many staircases are there at Hogwarts, the school featured in J. K. Rowling's Harry Potter books?"

NO! Not Harry Potter!

Owl, Dumbledore, magic wand, Hogwarts, cat, reading, map, Bubblehead, broomstick! Judy did backflips through her brain. Cartwheels in her cranium.

It was like her brain was speed-reading through the Harry Potter books, looking for an answer. Any answer.

It was no use. Judy had no idea what the answer was, but she dived for the buzzer anyway. Mighty Fantaskey beat her to it.

Oh, Scabbers! The Bookworms were going to lose now, and it would all be Judy's fault.

"One hundred and thirty-two," Mighty said without a blink or a pause.

"Sorry," said Mr Todd. "Incorrect."

WHAT?

Mighty the Fantastic Fourth-Grader had missed!

Half the crowd shouted "Ooh!" and "No-o!" Ms de la Cruz quietened them down.

Mr Todd turned to Judy. "Judy? Ten seconds. Do you have an answer?"

Judy froze. Numbers spun through her brain. *117! 256! 39!* Her mind was a muggle.

"Time," said Mr Todd. The Virginia Dare audience groaned. "The correct answer is one hundred and forty-two."

The audience leaned forward on the edges of their seats.

"For the win," said Ms de la Cruz. "Next question."

There was still a chance. Judy Moody, Super Book Whiz, to the rescue.

Yipes. Judy got a case of the Bookworm squirms. The bookworm shivers. The bookworm jitters. *Shake it off! Fake a cough!* Judy told herself.

She closed her eyes. She pictured the light-up Book Quiz Wizard's Cup in its place of honour – the glass case in the Virginia Dare School library.

Then it happened. Ms de la Cruz flipped to the next card. She looked at Judy and seemed like she was trying not to laugh as she asked the question: "What is Pippi Longstocking's full name?"

Pippi! Judy knew all things Pippi! Without missing a beat, she buzzed in. "Pippi ... uh ... Pippi..." Her mind went blank. She gulped. Brain freeze! *Tap-tap-tap.* She tapped her nose. She closed her eyes. She took a deep breath and then she spoke clearly into the microphone. "Pippilotta Delicatessa Windowshade Mackrelmint Ephraim's Daughter Long-stocking."

"That is correct!" said Ms de la Cruz.

"Woo-hoo!" The Bookworms jumped

and whooped and hollered and high-fived one another. "We did it!"

"Congratulations, Bookworms!" said Mr Todd.

The crowd erupted in noisy applause. Rocky whistled and Webster whooped. Mum and Dad hurried over to Judy and Stink. "Great job, kids." There were hugs all around.

When the excitement died down, the Bookworms shook hands with the Bloodsucking Fake-Mustache Defenders.

"Great game!" both teams agreed.

"We can hardly wait till next year," said a Fake-Mustache Defender.

"We're coming back, better than ever," said another. "Get ready."

"There's a new kid in town, and her name is Mighty Fantaskey!" said Mighty.

Third-Grade Something

A-ma-zing! The Bookworms had read their way to the finish. She, Judy Moody, could hardly believe they had won the first ever Book Quiz Blowout. *Uber*-rare!

Mr Todd presented the Bookworms with the light-up Book Quiz Wizard's Cup. It would soon take a place of honour in the glass case in the Virginia Dare School library. The whole school would be proud of the Bookworms.

Willa, the librarian from Virginia Dare, passed out backpacks to the kids on both teams. Each backpack had a book inside. Judy peeked inside and found her very own copy of *Charlotte's Web*.

"Hey, look," said Jessica Finch, showing Judy the inside front page. "It's signed by a pig!"

"That's Wilbur's auto-graph," said Judy, crack-ing up. Judy hugged the book to her. With or without a trophy, Judy was in a joyful-on-top-of-spaghetti mood. Because of the Book Quiz Blowout, she had discovered piles of new books. Aisles of new books.

Books.

She, Judy Moody, Bookworm, loved to read.

Webster's dad, Mr Gomez, tapped on the microphone. "We thank you all for coming and celebrating reading with us today. We hope both teams and their families and friends will stay for our Bowling Bash. I'm happy to announce that all proceeds today will be donated to Virginia Dare Elementary School and Braintree Academy, to help buy new books for their libraries."

Willa the librarian and a man from Braintree Academy stepped up to the front. Mr Gomez presented them with a giant cheque that was taller than Stink. It took two people just to hold it.

Judy could not believe her eyes. "Rare!" said Judy. "That's the biggest cheque I've ever seen!"

"One million dollars!" yelled Stink, jumping up and down.

Judy counted zeros. "It's one thou-

sand dollars, Stink. Each school gets five hundred dollars."

"Oops," said Stink. "Still. That's a lot of new books for the library!"

Judy pictured all the new books that would go to the library, with bright, shiny-clean covers and crackling spines. She imagined filling her backpack with brand-spanking-new, never-before-been-read books.

At last, Webster, the Bookworm mascot, yelled, "Taco time!" The Bookworms sat down with the Fake-Mustache Defenders. Everybody chatted excitedly about the game while they ate teeny-tiny pancake tacos. "And don't forget ice-cream tacos for dessert!" Webster told them.

Let the Book Quiz Bowling Bash begin!

Webster cranked up the music. The regular lights in the bowling alley went out. Sparkly disco lights came on. They flashed and twinkled across the ceiling like stars in the sky. The lanes pulsed with eerie neon colours. The bowling pins glowed zombie-green.

Glow-in-the-dark bowling! This was as spooky-exciting as reading about Pippi Longstocking bowling with ghosts in her attic. Cosmic!

Webster rolled the first ball. All the pins went tumbling down. Strike!

Mighty Fantaskey showed Judy Moody her glow-in-the-dark shoelaces. One of the Fake-Mustache Defenders bowled a spare.

Stink was happy when he didn't bowl a gutter ball! He was as jazzed as Trombone Shorty when he played the trombone.

The Bookworms could have bowled all day. The Bookworms could have bowled till midnight. Too bad midnight was way past their bedtime.

Judy felt like Tracy Beaker when she found a real home. She felt like Ada Twist, Scientist, when she made a way-important discovery.

Judy one-two-three hopped and kicked up her heels in a Pippi-Longstocking dance. *Tiddly-pom and piddly-dee!*

She, Judy Moody, Super Book Whiz, felt like the star of her own book – *Tales of a Third-Grade Something.*

Books referenced in
Judy Moody, Super Book Whiz,
listed alphabetically by title

8 Class Pets + 1 Squirrel ÷ 1 Dog = Chaos by
Vivian Vande Velde

The 13-Storey Treehouse by Andy Griffiths,
illustrated by Terry Denton

Ada Twist, Scientist by Andrea Beaty,
illustrated by David Roberts

Anna Hibiscus by Atinuke, illustrated by
Lauren Tobia

Artemis Fowl series by Eoin Colfer

Because of Winn-Dixie by Kate DiCamillo

Beezus and Ramona by Beverly Cleary

The Borrowers by Mary Norton

Charlie and the Chocolate Factory by Roald Dahl

Charlotte's Web by E. B. White

The Cherry Pie Princess by Vivian French

Cloudy with a Chance of Meatballs by Judith Barrett

Crayons Aren't for Eating by Ms Tater, the Crayon Lady (fictional title; find it in *Judy Moody Predicts the Future*)

Diary of a Spider by Doreen Cronin, illustrated by Harry Bliss

Dog Man by Dav Pilkey

El Deafo by Cece Bell

Emil and the Detectives by Erich Kästner

Encyclopedia Brown series by Donald J. Sobol

Escape from Mr Lemoncello's Library by Chris Grabenstein

Fake Mustache by Tom Angleberger

Fantastic Mr Fox by Roald Dahl

Julius Zebra: Grapple with the Greeks! by Gary
Northfield

Lassie series by Eric Knight

The Lion, the Witch and the Wardrobe
by C. S. Lewis

The Little Prince by Antoine de Saint-Exupéry

Lulu and the Duck in the Park by Hilary McKay

Mango and Bambang by Polly Faber

Merci Suárez Changes Gears by Meg Medina

Mercy Watson series by Kate DiCamillo,
illustrated by Chris Van Dusen

The Mousehole Cat by Antonia Barber

Mr Popper's Penguins by Richard and Florence
Atwater

Mrs Pepperpot Stories by Alf Proysen

My Father's Dragon by Ruth Stiles Gannett,
illustrated by Ruth Chrisman Gannett

The One and Only Ivan by Katherine Applegate

Pelé, King of Soccer / Pelé, El rey del fútbol by
Monica Brown, illustrated by Rudy Gutiérrez

Peppa Pig series, based on the TV series
created by Neville Astley and Mark Baker

Pippi Longstocking series by Astrid Lindgren

Pippi Longstocking by Astrid Lindgren

The Princess and the Crocodile by Laura Amy
Schlitz, illustrated by Brian Floca

The Princess in Black by Shannon and Dean
Hale, illustrated by LeUyen Pham

Ramona series by Beverly Cleary

Ratburger by David Walliams

Ribsy by Beverly Cleary

The Secret of Platform 13 by Eva Ibbotson

A Series of Unfortunate Events by Lemony
Snicket

Books referenced in
Judy Moody, Super Book Whiz,
listed by chapter and in order
of appearance

Chapter 1: Judy Longstocking

The Mousehole Cat

Inspector Flytrap

The World According to Humphrey

Juana & Lucas

Timmy Failure series

Silly Verses for Kids

Pippi Longstocking

El Deafo

Fake Mustache

Charlotte's Web

Harry Potter series

Tales of a Fourth Grade Nothing

The Mousehole Cat

Funnybones

Fantastic Mr Fox

The Princess and the Crocodile

Charlie and the Chocolate Factory

Chapter 2: A Bookworm Is Not a Worm

Tales of a Fourth Grade Nothing

Tom Gates: Dog Zombies Rule

Flat Stanley and the Magic Lamp

8 Class Pets + 1 Squirrel ÷ 1 Dog = Chaos

The Infamous Ratsos

Mrs Pepperpot series

Crayons Aren't for Eating by Ms Tater, the Crayon
   Lady (fictional title; find it in *Judy Moody
   Predicts the Future*)

Chapter 3: Unicorns Don't Wear Trousers

The Princess in Black

Harry Potter and the Deathly Hallows

Harry Potter and the Order of the Phoenix

Beezus and Ramona

Chapter 4: Goldfish Thinking

Peppa Pig series

Anna Hibiscus

Mr Popper's Penguins

Lassie series

Because of Winn-Dixie

The Mousehole Cat

Ivy and Bean: No News Is Good News

Tintin and the Lake of Sharks

The Cherry Pie Princess

The Borrowers

Cloudy with a Chance of Meatballs

Tales of a Fourth Grade Nothing

Charlie and the Chocolate Factory

Harry Potter series

Chapter 5: Brain Freeze

The 13-Storey Treehouse

Mango and Bambang

Diary of a Spider

Emil and the Detectives

Lulu and the Duck in the Park

My Father's Dragon

Encyclopedia Brown series

Chapter 6: Grumpy Bacon

The One and Only Ivan

Pippi Longstocking series

Mercy Watson series

Charlotte's Web

Ramona series

Horrid Henry series

Merci Suárez Changes Gears

Escape from Mr Lemoncello's Library

Mr Popper's Penguins

Charlie and the Chocolate Factory

Horrid Henry's Underpants

Julius Zebra: Grapple with the Greeks!

Chapter 7: The Mighty Fourth-Grader

Tales of a Fourth Grade Nothing

Encyclopedia Brown series

Harry Potter and the Order of the Phoenix

The Infamous Ratsos

The Borrowers

Charlotte's Web

Pippi Longstocking series

Chapter 8: Super Book Whiz

The Princess in Black

El Deafo

Tales of a Fourth Grade Nothing

Ratburger

Pippi Longstocking

Mr Popper's Penguins

Chapter 9: Bookworms vs. Bloodsucking Fake-Mustache Defenders

Ada Twist, Scientist

The Tail of Emily Windsnap

Charlotte's Web

A Series of Unfortunate Events

Artemis Fowl series

Stuart Little

James and the Giant Peach

The Story of Tracy Beaker

Because of Winn-Dixie

The Winnie-the-Pooh series

Dog Man

The Little Prince

Charlie and the Chocolate Factory

The Lion, the Witch and the Wardrobe

Pelé, King of Soccer / Pelé, El rey del fútbol

Trombone Shorty

The Secret of Platform 13

Escape from Mr Lemoncello's Library

Harry Potter series

Pippi Longstocking series

Chapter 10: Third-Grade Something

Charlotte's Web

Pippi Longstocking

Trombone Shorty

The Story of Tracy Beaker

Ada Twist, Scientist

photo by Michele McDonald

Megan McDonald is the author of the popular Judy Moody and Stink series, as well as the Judy Moody and Friends series for new readers. She has written many other books for children, including the Ant and Honey Bee stories, the Sisters Club series and several picture books. Before she began writing full-time, Megan McDonald worked as a librarian, a bookseller and a living-history actress. She lives in Northern California, USA, with her husband, Richard Haynes, who is also a writer.

Peter H. Reynolds is the illustrator of the popular Judy Moody and Stink series in addition to many other books, including several for which he is also author.

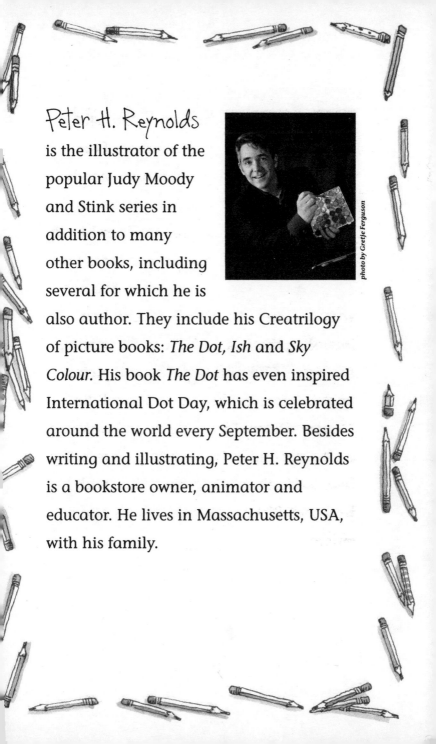

photo by Gretje Ferguson

They include his Creatrilogy of picture books: *The Dot, Ish* and *Sky Colour*. His book *The Dot* has even inspired International Dot Day, which is celebrated around the world every September. Besides writing and illustrating, Peter H. Reynolds is a bookstore owner, animator and educator. He lives in Massachusetts, USA, with his family.